RUDOLPH'S NIGHT OFF
BY BAXTER BLACK
ILLUSTRATED BY BILL PATTERSON

Copyright ©2011 by Baxter Black

Published by: Coyote Cowboy Company
PO Box 2190
Benson, AZ 85602
baxterblack.com
All rights reserved

Cover and book design by Becky Harvey

LIBRARY OF CONGRESS CATALOGING IN PUBLICATION DATA:
Main entry under:
Cowboy Poetry

Bibliography: p
1. Rudolph's Night Off
2. Christmas
3. Cowboy-Poetry

I. Black, Baxter, 1945-
Library of Congress #2011911207
ISBN-13: 978-0-939343-54-6

OTHER BOOKS BY BAXTER
The Cowboy and His Dog
A Rider, A Roper, And A Heck'uva Windmill Man
On The Edge Of Common Sense, The Best So Far
Doc, While Yer Here
Buckaroo History
Coyote Cowboy Poetry
Croutons On A Cow Pie
The Buckskin Mare
Cowboy Standard Time
Croutons On A Cow Pie, Vol 2
Hey, Cowboy, Wanna Get Lucky? (Crown Publishing, Inc.)
Dunny And The Duck
Cow Attack
Cactus Tracks And Cowboy Philosophy (Crown Publishing, Inc.)
A Cowful Of Cowboy Poetry
Horseshoes, Cowsocks And Duckfeet (Crown Publishing, Inc.)
Ag Man The Comic Book
Hey, Cowgirl, Need A Ride? (Crown Publishing, Inc.)
Blazin' Bloats & Cows On Fire!
The World According To Baxter Black: Quips, Quirks & Quotes
The Back Page (Western Horseman Books)
Lessons From A Desperado Poet (TwoDot Publishing)

'TWAS THE NIGHT BEFORE CHRISTMAS
AND RUDOLPH WAS LAME!
THE VET FROM THE NORTH POLE
SAID, "FOOTROT'S TO BLAME

I'LL GIVE HIM SOME SULFA,
IT'S THE BEST I CAN DO
BUT STALL REST IS NEEDED
THE NEXT WEEK OR TWO."

"No cop in his right mind would give any clout to a geezer who claimed that his reindeer went out!"

HE GATHERED THE OTHERS, OL' DONNER AND BLITZEN,

WERE ANY AMONG 'EM WHOSE NOSE WAS TRANSMITZEN?

OMMM

THEY GRUNTED AND STRAINED

AND SURE MADE A MESS!

BUT NO NOSES GLOWED BRIGHTLY

OR EARS LUMINESCED.

WHEN UP STEPPED OL' BILLY,
THE GOAT FROM LAMPASAS.

HE SHIVERED AND SHOOK
LIKE A MOUSE ON THE ARK
BUT HIS HORNS WERE A BEACON . . .
THEY GLOWED IN THE DARK!

SANTY WENT CRAZY!
HE ASKED, "WHY?"
WITH A SMILE

"I just ate a watch
with a radium dial!

Where I come from in Texas
we don't have thick hide
My skin is so thin
it shines through from inside."

"If that's true then let's feed him!"
cried Santy with glee
"Gather everything burnin'
and bring it to me!"

So Billy ate flashbulbs
and solar collectors,
Electrical eels
and road sign reflectors,

FIRECRACKER SPARKLERS, A LADY SCHICK SHAVER
AND LIFESAVERS, ALL OF EM' Wintergreen FLAVOR,

JELLY FROM **phosphorescellous fish,**

DAY GLOW PIZZA IN A glittering DISH,

FIREFLIES AND CANDLES

AND STUFF THAT IGNITES,

THEN HAD HIM A BIG BOWL OF
NORTHERING LIGHTS!

He danced on the rug and petted the cat
And after he'd finished and done all of that
To store up the static 'lectricity better
They forced him to eat two balloons

and a SWEATER!

THEN HE OPENED
HIS MOUTH, LIGHT
FELL THE FLOOR

LIKE THE FRIDGE
LIGHT COMES ON
WHEN YOU OPEN
THE DOOR!

HIS HALLOWEEN SMILE COULDN'T BE BETTER DRAWN
WHEN HE BURPED, ACCIDENTLY,
HIS HIGH BEAMS KICKED ON!

"HITCH HIM UP!" CRIED OL' SANTY,
AND THEY WENT ON THEIR WAY.

I REMEMBER THAT CHRISTMAS
TO THIS VERY DAY.

THE SKY WAS ABLAZE
WITH THE STARS SHINING BRIGHT.
THEY WERE SHOOTING AND

FALLING

ALL THROUGH THE NIGHT.

AND I REALIZE NOW,
THOUGH MY FINGERS ARE CROSSED
WHAT I REALLY WAS SEEIN'...
WAS OL' BILLY'S EXHAUST!

THE END

☆ BAXTER ☆ BLACK ☆

For as long as he can remember, Baxter's family has shared a tradition on Christmas Eve. It includes reading the scripture from Matthew and Luke describing the birth of Christ and the three wise men. Children on hand enact the story with Nativity scene figurines, sometimes substituting Long-horn cattle, cowboys on horseback, and Army tanks or Barbie Dolls when needed. A prayer is said and *Silent Night* is sung. Then, *The Night Before Christmas*, by Clement Moore is recited, verse by verse, around the circle by memory.

Baxter says he can not remember a single Christmas Eve when the communal poetry recitation did not end in chaos! "... dry leaves prancing and pawing more rapid than eagles hit by a wild hurricane rose up the chimney like the down of a thistle ..." till eventually somebody turned like a jerk and threw up the sash!

With apologies to Mr. Moore, Dr. Black wrote his own version. And yes, being the former large animal veterinarian he is, he does realize goats do not have upper incisors. But, Mr. Patterson, the artist, insisted that if poets can make translucent flying goats, then artists can bestow upon the creature an upper plate! How else, he reasoned, could Billy from Lampasas eat a light bulb?

Baxter dedicates this book to all the kids who still believe that goats are wired for 220 watts and reindeer can fly.

Bill Patterson graduated from the University of Tulsa. As owner of his own art and design studio for 35 years, he illustrates annual reports and corporate image materials . . . and more recently gleaming goats.

As a fine art painter, he has shown works at the Gilcrease Museum American Art in Miniature Show, the Kentucky Derby Museum of Art, and the Pierson Gallery, Tulsa. One of his areas of interest is in equestrian (and now, radiant Capra Hircus) art. A selection of these works were shown in the Remington Gallery in Oklahoma City.

Living in Tucson, AZ for several years gave Bill the opportunity to study and paint the surrounding desert and other areas of the Southwest. Now living in Oklahoma, Bill continues to paint representational and interpretive examples of that subject matter.

Bill
Patterson

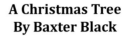

A Christmas Tree
By Baxter Black

A Christmas tree is one of those things
Like popcorn balls or angel wings
That children make in the snow.

Things with beauty unsurpassed
That touch our lives but never last
More than a week or so.

It shines from every living room
Like someone in a bright costume
That's happy to see you drop by.

And in a world that never slows down
To see their lights all over town
Warms you up inside.

And it's nice to get to know one well
To know each tinsel and jingle bell
That often as not don't ring.

I can stare at the lights and never stop
Look back at the angel up on the top
And imagine he can sing.

Even the scraggliest Christmas tree
Seems to have some dignity
Guarding the gifts below.

But all the ones I've seen up close
Seem to be smiling and acting the host
To all who say hello.

Sometimes I think, if I were a tree
The most that I could hope to be
is one of those wonderful pines.

That gets to spend a week with friends
When even a grown-up kid pretends
That all the world is fine.